Turn on the TV

by Justine Ciovacco

BLACKBIRCH PRESS

THOMSON
GALE

San Diego • Detroit • New York • San Francisco • Cleveland • New Haven, Conn. • Waterville, Maine • London • Munich

THOMSON
★
GALE

© 2004 by Blackbirch Press™. Blackbirch Press™ is an imprint of The Gale Group, Inc., a division of Thomson Learning, Inc.

Blackbirch Press™ and Thomson Learning™ are trademarks used herein under license.

For more information, contact
The Gale Group, Inc.
27500 Drake Rd.
Farmington Hills, MI 48331-3535
Or you can visit our Internet site at http://www.gale.com

ALL RIGHTS RESERVED
No part of this work covered by the copyright hereon may be reproduced or used in any form or by any means—graphic, electronic, or mechanical, including photocopying, recording, taping, Web distribution or information storage retrieval systems—without the written permission of the publisher.

Every effort has been made to trace the owners of copyrighted material.

Photo Credits: see page 47.

LIBRARY OF CONGRESS CATALOGING-IN-PUBLICATION DATA

Ciovacco, Justine.
 Turn on the TV / by Justine Ciovacco.
  p. cm. — (Step back science series)
Includes index.
Summary: Explains what happens when a television is turned on using a remote control device and describing how images and sounds are transmitted and received.
 ISBN 1-56711-680-9 (hardback : alk. paper)
 1. Television—Juvenile literature. [1. Television.] I. Title. II. Series.

TK6640 .C567 2003
621.388—dc21   2002013162

Printed in United States
10 9 8 7 6 5 4 3 2 1

Contents

Turn on the TV

Turn on the TV 6
How does a TV work?

Images Appear on Screen 8
What makes the images show up on the screen?

Light Rays Form Inside TV 10
Where do the electrons come from?

Electricity Provides Heat to TV as Receiver Picks Up Signal ... 12
What heats the cathode?

▶ **SIDE STEP: In Control** 14
How does a remote control turn on the TV?

Large Broadcast Dishes Send Signals to Home-Based Receivers ... 16
How do TV signals reach home-based receivers across the country?

▶ **SIDE STEP: Cable's Stable** 18
Why is a cable connection the fastest way to get a TV signal?

Space Satellites Bounce Signals Back to Earth 20
Where do the large broadcast dishes get their signals?

Transmitters Send Signals to Satellites 22
How do the radio-wave signals get to the satellite?

Wires Send Signals to Transmitter 24
How do the electrical TV signals get to the transmitter?

Master Control Room Sends Signals out of TV Station 26
Where in the TV station do the transmitter's signals come from?

Three Control Rooms Send Signals to Master Control Room 28
Where do the signals produced in the master control room come from?

Director Calls Shots from Production Control Room 30
Who decides what will be seen and heard?

In-Studio Cameras Film Action on Set 32
How do these in-studio cameras record action?

Microphones Record Sound 34
How is sound recorded in a TV studio?

▶ **SIDE STEP: Remote Control** 36
How is the creation of video footage different outside a studio?

Set Designed for Broadcasts to Start on Director's Call 38
Where in a TV studio are the picture and sound produced?

The Big Picture 40
Explore the science behind turning on the TV, step by step.

Facts and Figures 42
Seen and Heard

Wonders and Words 44
Questions and Answers

Glossary 45

Index 46

For More Information 48

How to Use This Book

Each Step Back Science book traces the path of a science-based act backwards, from its result to its beginning.

Each double-page spread like the ones below explains one step in the process.

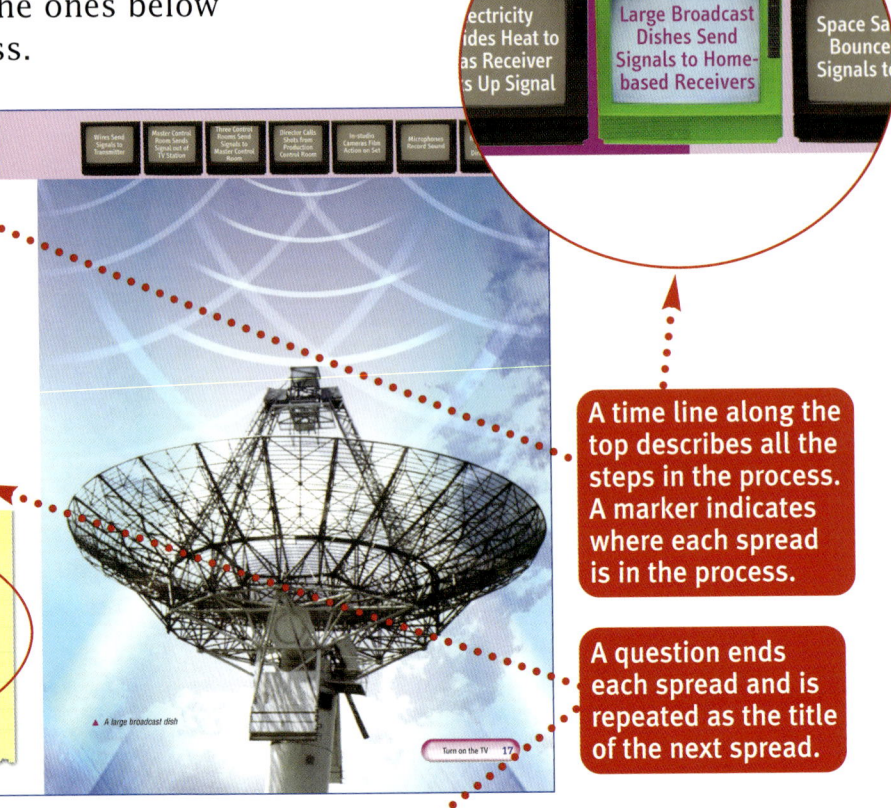

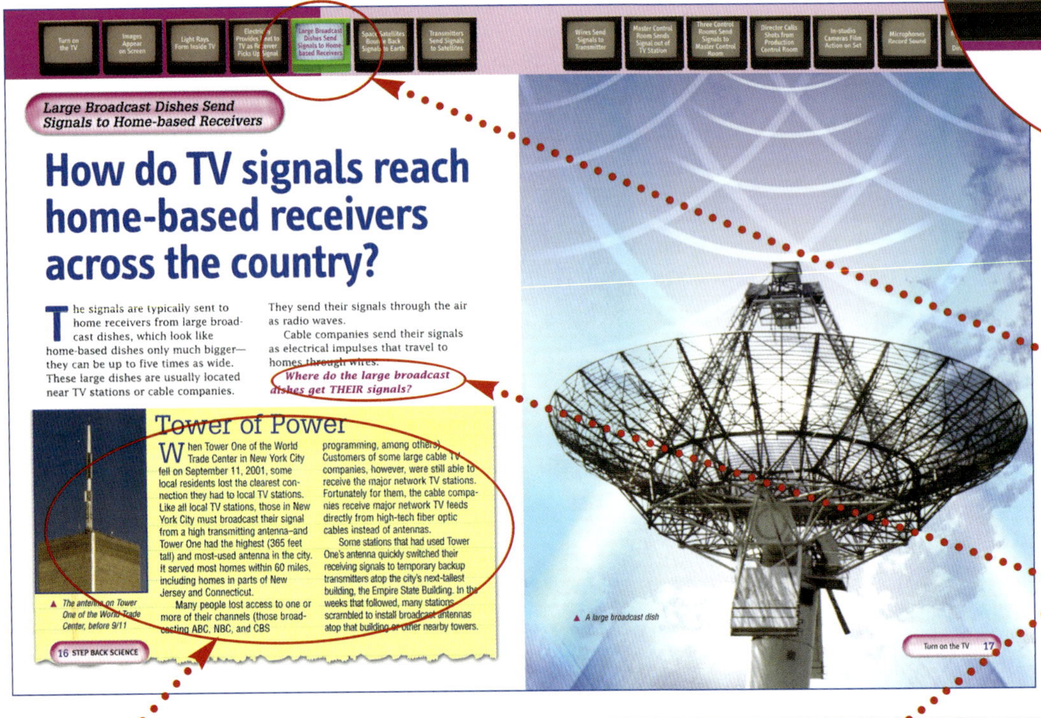

A time line along the top describes all the steps in the process. A marker indicates where each spread is in the process.

A question ends each spread and is repeated as the title of the next spread.

Sidebars show interesting related information.

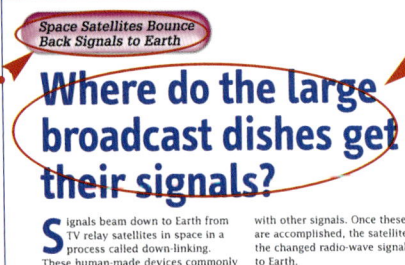

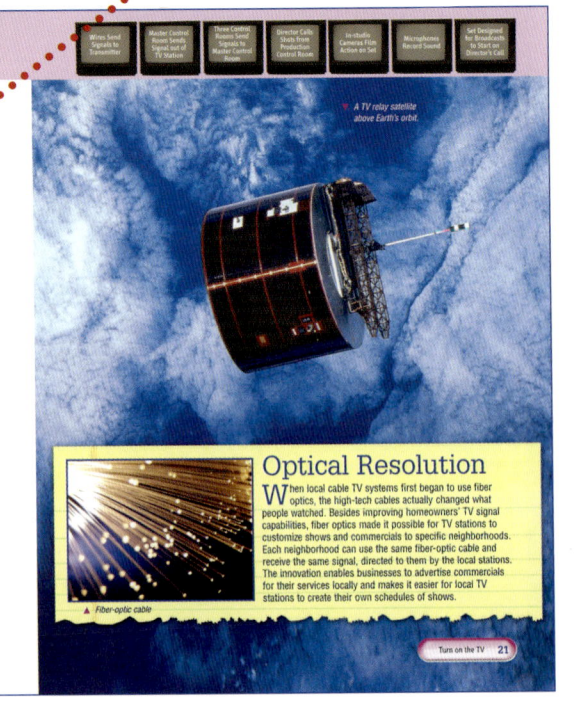

A short description gives a quick answer to the question asked at the end of the previous step.

4 STEP BACK SCIENCE

Side Step spreads, like the one below, offer separate but related information.

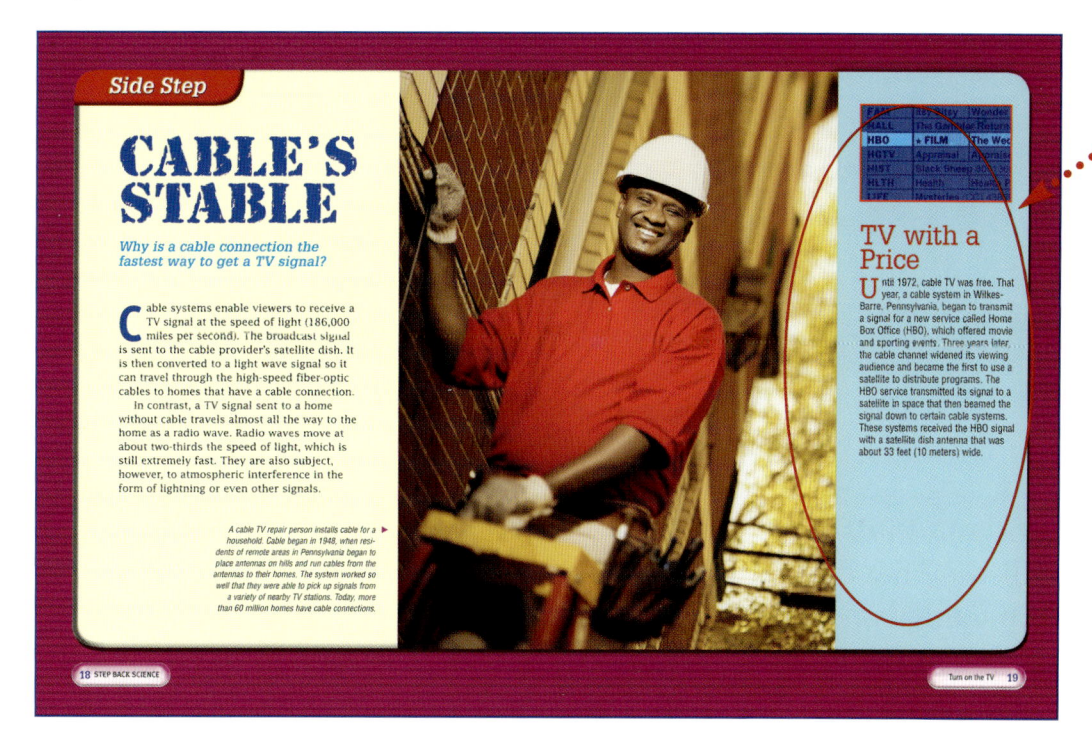

Every Side Step spread contains a sidebar.

The Big Picture, on pages 40–41, shows you the entire process at a glance.

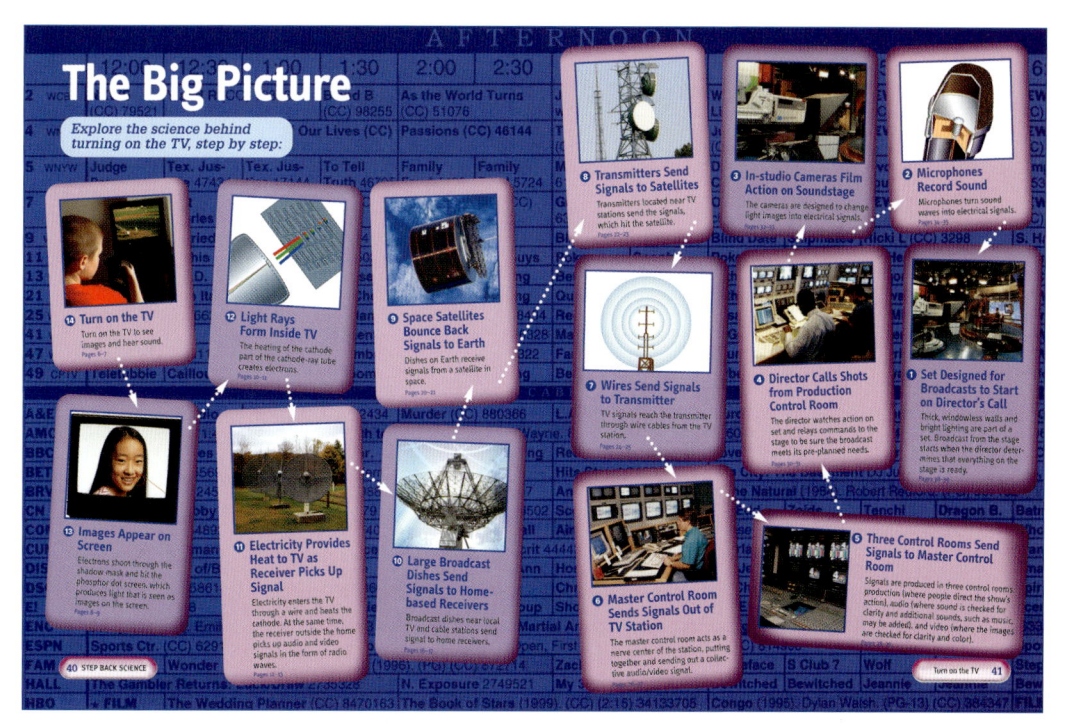

Turn on the TV 5

| Turn on the TV | Images Appear on Screen | Light Rays Form Inside TV | Electricity Provides Heat to TV as Receiver Picks Up Signal | Large Broadcast Dishes Send Signals to Home-Based Receivers | Space Satellites Bounce Back Signals to Earth | Transmitters Send Signals to Satellites |

Turn on the TV

How does a TV work?

Thanks to television, people can have entertainment and information at their fingertips. All they have to do is press a button, and the TV comes on to open a world of pictures and sounds created for their enjoyment and education.

What goes on behind the screen and behind the scenes? The TV set has its own electronic inner workings. A lot of what makes the experience possible, however, happens at a TV station. The station relays signals in the form of broadcast waves to the set through a network of earthbound transmitters and receivers and space-based satellites.

Step through the images on the screen and explore the amazing series of events that makes TV a reality, starting with:

What makes the images show up on the screen?

| Wires Send Signals to Transmitter | Master Control Room Sends Signals out of TV Station | Three Control Rooms Send Signals to Master Control Room | Director Calls Shots from Production Control Room | In-Studio Cameras Film Action on Set | Microphones Record Sound | Set Designed for Broadcasts to Start on Director's Call |

Turn on the TV   7

Images Appear on Screen

What makes the images show up on the screen?

The TV screen is not just a piece of glass. It contains thousands of dots made of chemicals called phosphors. Each dot contains a red, blue, or green phosphor. When the TV is turned on, the phosphors are hit by beams of electrons traveling at a high speed from behind the screen. This causes them to glow. Every second, the entire screen is swept top to bottom by electrons thirty times.

The electrons are shot through a metal grille called the shadow mask, behind the TV screen. The holes in the shadow mask line up the beams of electrons with the right color dots. Because the dots are so small and there are so many of them, we see colors when combinations of the dots glow at once. The dots are so close together that the human brain reads them as a single image. The image changes every fraction of a second as the dots are continually hit by electrons, varying their color and intensity.

But where do the electrons come from?

STEP BACK SCIENCE

| Wires Send Signals to Transmitter | Master Control Room Sends Signals out of TV Station | Three Control Rooms Send Signals to Master Control Room | Director Calls Shots from Production Control Room | In-Studio Cameras Film Action on Set | Microphones Record Sound | Set Designed for Broadcasts to Start on Director's Call |

▲ Images that appear on the TV screen are made up of combinations of dots.

The Dark Side

When the public began to buy TVs in the 1940s, they had only one viewing option: black and white. Instead of multi-colored phosphor dots, black-and-white TVs have screens coated with a single sheet of phosphor that only produces white light.

Inside the TV, the cathode-ray tube creates only one beam of electrons. Because the lines of phosphor dots are so close, the human brain reads them as single images in shades of black, white, and gray.

Today, some small TVs are still made for black-and-white images. They receive the same outside electrical signals that color TVs pick up, but they are designed to ignore the parts of the signals that indicate which colors should be on-screen.

▲ A very early TV

Turn on the TV 9

| Turn on the TV | Images Appear on Screen | **Light Rays Form Inside TV** | Electricity Provides Heat to TV as Receiver Picks Up Signal | Large Broadcast Dishes Send Signals to Home-Based Receivers | Space Satellites Bounce Back Signals to Earth | Transmitters Send Signals to Satellites |

Light Rays Form Inside TV

Where do the electrons come from?

The electrons are shot through three electron guns. The guns are fired from the back of the cathode-ray tube, also called a picture tube because it produces the electrons that create the moving pictures. This airtight glass tube contains a heated filament called the cathode, which, like the filament in a lightbulb, gets so hot that it produces a strong beam of electrons. These electrons are focused by magnets inside the cathode-ray tube and sent in beams toward the shadow mask.

So what heats the cathode?

Going with the Flow

In the early 1900s, the use of vacuum tubes was the only way to increase and direct signals in electronic telecommunications. These were airtight glass tubes through which electricity flowed. Although hailed as a technological marvel, they were unreliable, expensive to produce, and used a lot of energy. By the mid-1940s, three scientists at Bell Telephone Laboratories in Murray Hill, New Jersey, were working to develop a device to replace vacuum tubes.

The physics experts—John Bardeen, Walter Brattain, and William Shockley—created the transistor, which changed communications forever. They sandwiched crystals made of the metal-like element germanium between two metal plates and added an electrical current. Their design allows electricity to flow through the device and act as a switch, using a small amount of electricity to control the gateway to a much larger supply of electricity.

"Asking us to predict what transistors will do," said one excited fellow engineer upon the invention's public unveiling in 1948, "is like asking the man who first put wheels on an ox cart to foresee the automobile, the wristwatch, or the high speed generator." The scientists were awarded the Nobel Prize in physics in 1956.

| Wires Send Signals to Transmitter | Master Control Room Sends Signals out of TV Station | Three Control Rooms Send Signals to Master Control Room | Director Calls Shots from Production Control Room | In-Studio Cameras Film Action on Set | Microphones Record Sound | Set Designed for Broadcasts to Start on Director's Call |

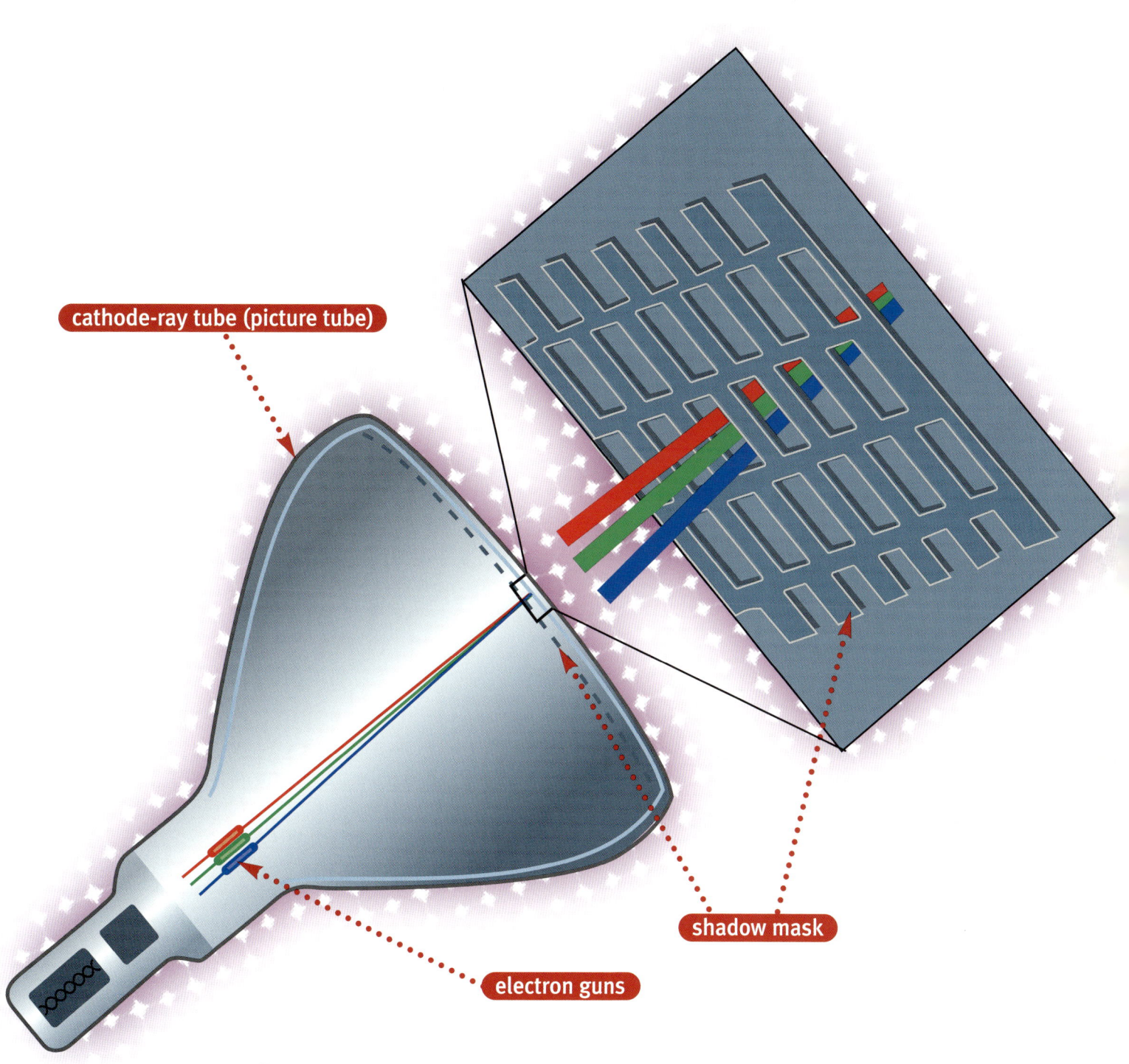

- **cathode-ray tube (picture tube)**
- **shadow mask**
- **electron guns**

▲ *Three guns shoot electrons through the picture tube and shadow mask at red, blue, and green phosphor dots.*

Turn on the TV **11**

Electricity Provides Heat to TV as Receiver Picks Up Signal

What heats the cathode?

Electricity—a flow of excited electrons—traveling through a home's wiring system creates the heat. When viewers turn on the TV set, they open a passageway that allows electricity to flow from the wires in the walls to the wires in the back of the TV and through the set itself.

Electricity alone, however, cannot create pictures and sound. The TV needs not only to be plugged in and turned on, it also needs to receive a broadcast signal. Picture (video) and sound (audio) signals arrive as one unified signal, either by a home-based receiver or by a TV cable. The receiver is typically a metal antenna or a bowl-shaped satellite dish that is placed on top of or near the home. It receives signals as radio waves that move through the air. The signals are carried into a home through wires.

The receiver separates the audio and video signals, ensuring that the audio signal moves to the TV's loudspeaker at the same time the video signal goes to the TV's cathode-ray tube.

Homes using cable do not need receivers. Fiber-optic cables carry TV signals into these homes. These cables are razor-thin glass or plastic tubes that can transmit large amounts of information as pulses of light. A single fiber-optic cable can serve as many as five hundred homes, and because they are so thin, bunches can be bundled to provide millions of homes with powerful TV signals.

How do TV signals reach home-based receivers across the country?

STEP BACK SCIENCE

| Wires Send Signals to Transmitter | Master Control Room Sends Signals out of TV Station | Three Control Rooms Send Signals to Master Control Room | Director Calls Shots from Production Control Room | In-Studio Cameras Film Action on Set | Microphones Record Sound | Set Designed for Broadcasts to Start on Director's Call |

▲ *Satellite dishes receive TV signals as radio waves.*

Making News

Only a few people saw one of the most famous TV shows in American history. Television cameras from RCA/NBC rolled in April 1939 as President Franklin D. Roosevelt became the star of the first TV news event: a live show about the opening ceremonies of the New York World's Fair in Schenectady, New York. Only a few TV stations in New York City that were ready to pick up the signal were able to broadcast the show.

◀ *Washington, D.C., September 1942. Early in TV's history, a broadcast announced the formation of a high school victory corps throughout the United States. The broadcast was made over station WMAL from 8:30 to 9:00 P.M.*

Turn on the TV 13

Side Step

IN CONTROL

How does a remote control turn on the TV?

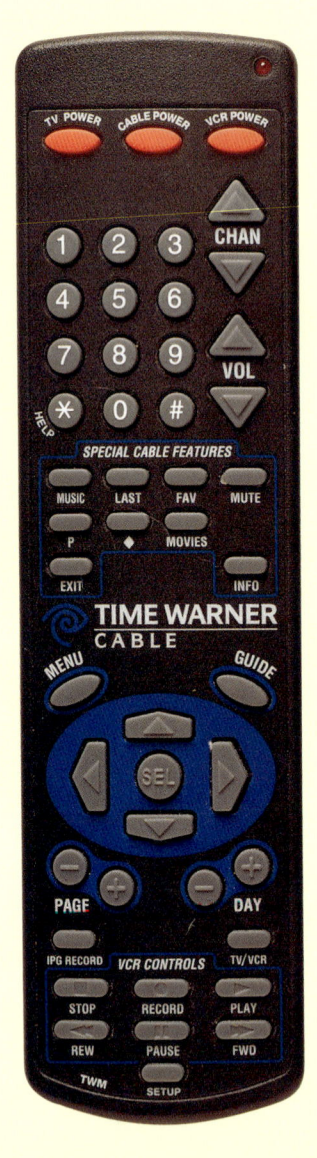

▲ Battery-powered remote control devices translate an electrical signal from the on-off button into a radio signal that hits the TV.

14 STEP BACK SCIENCE

The remote uses radio waves to control TV functions. Powered by electricity from batteries, the remote control translates the button you press on its surface into signals that can be understood by the TV set.

Here is how it works: A person aims the remote at the TV—actually at a flat sensor that is located near the TV screen—and presses the rubber button that says "Power/On." This action completes an electrical circuit that causes electricity to flow though a thin fiberglass circuit board inside the remote.

An electrical chip on the board receives the electrical signal from the on-off button and translates it into a radio signal that is unique for the receiver on that particular TV. This signal leaves the remote and hits the receptor on the TV.

▲ New York City's Empire State Building

Broadcast Beginnings

Without radio, there may have been no TV. Television stations depend on radio waves to send out signals, and many radio stations helped fund their TV counterparts. For example, NBC began to transmit experimental broadcasts that featured cartoon character Felix the Cat from New York's Empire State Building as early as 1932. By 1935, the company was spending millions of dollars a year on television research, and it was all paid for by the income of the then-popular NBC radio networks.

| Turn on the TV | Images Appear on Screen | Light Rays Form Inside TV | Electricity Provides Heat to TV as Receiver Picks Up Signal | **Large Broadcast Dishes Send Signals to Home-Based Receivers** | Space Satellites Bounce Back Signals to Earth | Transmitters Send Signals to Satellites |

Large Broadcast Dishes Send Signals to Home-Based Receivers

How do TV signals reach home-based receivers across the country?

The signals are typically sent to home receivers from large broadcast dishes, which look like home-based dishes only much bigger—they can be up to five times as wide. These large dishes are usually located near TV stations or cable companies. TV stations send their signals through the air as radio waves. Cable companies send their signals as electrical impulses that travel to homes through wires.

Where do the large broadcast dishes get their signals?

Tower of Power

When Tower One of the World Trade Center in New York City fell on September 11, 2001, some local residents lost the clearest connection they had to local TV stations. Like all local TV stations, those in New York City must broadcast their signals from a high transmitting antenna—and Tower One had the highest (365 feet tall) and most-used antenna in the city. It served most homes within 60 miles, including homes in parts of New Jersey and Connecticut.

Many people lost access to one or more of their channels (those broadcasting programming for ABC, NBC, and CBS, among others). Customers of some large cable TV companies, however, were still able to receive the major network TV stations. Fortunately for them, the cable companies receive major network TV feeds directly from high-tech fiber-optic cables instead of antennas.

Some stations that had used Tower One's antenna quickly switched their receiving signals to temporary backup transmitters atop the city's next-tallest building, the Empire State Building. In the weeks that followed, many stations scrambled to install broadcast antennas atop that building or other nearby towers.

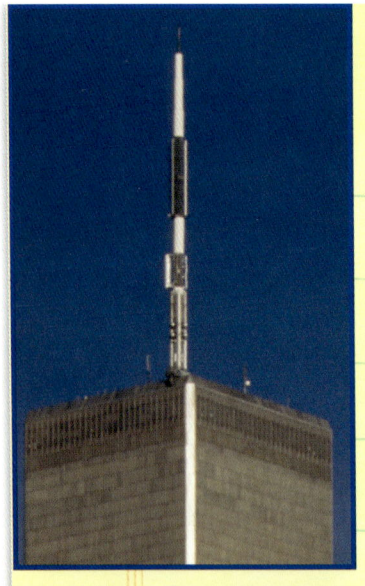

▲ Tower One of the World Trade Center featured a huge antenna.

16 STEP BACK SCIENCE

| Wires Send Signals to Transmitter | Master Control Room Sends Signals out of TV Station | Three Control Rooms Send Signals to Master Control Room | Director Calls Shots from Production Control Room | In-Studio Cameras Film Action on Set | Microphones Record Sound | Set Designed for Broadcasts to Start on Director's Call |

▲ TV stations and cable companies use large broadcast dishes to distribute their signals.

Turn on the TV 17

Side Step

CABLE'S STABLE

Why is a cable connection the fastest way to get a TV signal?

Cable systems enable viewers to receive a TV signal at the speed of light (186,000 miles per second). The broadcast signal is sent to the cable provider's satellite dish. It is then converted to a light wave signal so it can travel through the high-speed fiber-optic cables to homes that have a cable connection.

In contrast, a TV signal sent to a home without cable travels almost all the way to the home as a radio wave. Radio waves move at about two-thirds the speed of light, which is still extremely fast. They are also subject, however, to atmospheric interference in the form of lightning or even other signals.

▶ A cable TV repair person installs cable for a household. Cable began in 1948, when residents of remote areas in Pennsylvania began to place antennas on hills and run cables from the antennas to their homes. The system worked so well that they were able to pick up signals from a variety of nearby TV stations. Today, more than 60 million homes have cable connections.

18 STEP BACK SCIENCE

TV with a Price

Until 1972, cable TV was free. That year, a cable system in Wilkes-Barre, Pennsylvania, began to transmit a signal for a new service called Home Box Office (HBO), which offered movie and sporting events. Three years later, the cable channel widened its viewing audience and became the first to use a satellite to distribute programs. The HBO service transmitted its signal to a satellite in space that then beamed the signal down to certain cable systems. These systems received the HBO signal with a satellite dish antenna that was about 33 feet (10 meters) wide.

Turn on the TV 19

Space Satellites Bounce Signals Back to Earth

Where do the large broadcast dishes get their signals?

Signals beam down to Earth from TV relay satellites in space in a process called down-linking. These human-made devices commonly float in orbits 22,300 miles above Earth. They receive TV signals as radio waves broadcast, or transmitted, from Earth. They then amplify, or increase, the signal. At the same time, they change each wave's frequency—the amount of time a wave moves up and down per second—so it does not mix with other signals. Once these tasks are accomplished, the satellites send the changed radio-wave signals back to Earth.

Satellites orbit Earth at the same speed at which the planet is rotating. This enables the satellites to keep the same position above Earth, so TV signals can locate them.

But how do the radio-wave signals get to the satellite?

20 STEP BACK SCIENCE

| Wires Send Signals to Transmitter | Master Control Room Sends Signals out of TV Station | Three Control Rooms Send Signals to Master Control Room | Director Calls Shots from Production Control Room | In-Studio Cameras Film Action on Set | Microphones Record Sound | Set Designed for Broadcasts to Start on Director's Call |

▼ *A TV relay satellite orbiting Earth.*

Optical Resolution

When local cable TV systems first began to use fiber optics, the high-tech cables actually changed what people watched. Besides improving homeowners' TV signal capabilities, fiber optics made it possible for TV stations to customize shows and commercials to specific neighborhoods. Each neighborhood can use the same fiber-optic cable and receive the same signal, directed to them by the local stations. The innovation enables businesses to advertise commercials for their services locally and makes it easier for local TV stations to create their own schedules of shows.

▲ *Fiber-optic cable*

Turn on the TV 21

| Turn on the TV | Images Appear on Screen | Light Rays Form Inside TV | Electricity Provides Heat to TV as Receiver Picks Up Signal | Large Broadcast Dishes Send Signals to Home-Based Receivers | Space Satellites Send Signals to Broadcast Dishes | **Transmitters Send Signals to Satellites** |

Transmitters Send Signals to Satellites

How do the radio-wave signals get to the satellite?

Satellites above Earth pick up, or up-link, TV signals in the form of radio waves from transmitters located near the TV stations. These tall transmitters convert signals sent in an electrical format from the station into radio waves. The format change enables the signals to move through the air, into space, as radio waves. Because signals lose power as they move away from their source, transmitters are equipped with amplifiers to strengthen the waves they send to distant satellites.

So how do the electrical TV signals get to the transmitter?

Fine Tuning TV

Digital TV (DTV) was created to improve upon analog TV—the kind used since the 1950s. Digital TV sets display images that are clearer than ever before because they have twice as many phosphor lines to scan as other TVs. The sharper images are also due in part to the coding system used by DTV sets. Just like DVDs and compact discs, these TV sets receive information as a series of codes, using the digits "0" and "1." The system for decoding these signals takes up less space than the system for decoding electrical signals.

A DTV set works best when paired with digital TV signals, a special format that must come from the TV stations. When both digital elements are used, the result is CD-quality sound and TV images that are wider and up to ten times as sharp as analog. By 2006, the Federal Communications Commission (FCC)—a government agency that oversees the communications industry—has ruled that all TV stations should begin to use digital broadcasts. That means that by 2006, all analog TV set owners must buy DTVs, or buy set-top boxes that will make digital TV signals readable for their current TVs.

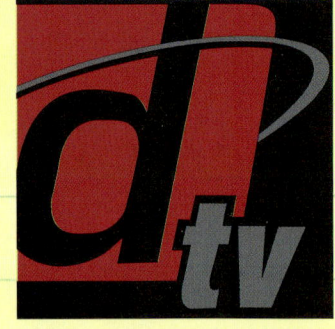

22 STEP BACK SCIENCE

| Wires Send Signals to Transmitter | Master Control Room Sends Signals out of TV Station | Three Control Rooms Send Signals to Master Control Room | Director Calls Shots from Production Control Room | In-Studio Cameras Film Action on Set | Microphones Record Sound | Set Designed for Broadcasts to Start on Director's Call |

▲ *Tall transmitters convert electrical signals sent from a TV station into radio waves.*

Turn on the TV **23**

| Turn on the TV | Images Appear on Screen | Light Rays Form Inside TV | Electricity Provides Heat to TV as Receiver Picks Up Signal | Large Broadcast Dishes Send Signals to Home-Based Receivers | Space Satellites Send Signals to Broadcast Dishes | Transmitters Send Signals to Satellites |

Wires Send Signals to Transmitter

How do the electrical TV signals get to the transmitter?

An electrical TV signal reaches the transmitter through wires from the nearby TV station. The signal sent from the station is not simply an audio/video signal. It also includes travel information and special decoding instructions. This ensures that only certain transmitters and receivers pick up the signals. It is illegal for owners of other transmitters and receivers to pick up signals they do not have permission to use. If they try to do so, the process is often blocked by the secret coding information.

Where in the TV station do the transmitter's signals come from?

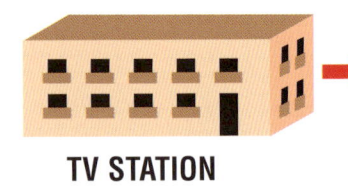

TV STATION → **OSCILLATOR** → **MODULATOR** → **AMPLIFIER** →

First, a device called an oscillator creates a carrier signal—the "blank page" on which the audio/video information will be written.

Second, a modulator encodes the carrier signal with the audio/video information from the TV station.

Finally, an amplifier strengthens the signal until it is powerful enough to be received by satellites.

24 Step Back Science

| Wires Send Signals to Transmitter | Master Control Room Sends Signals out of TV Station | Three Control Rooms Send Signals to Master Control Room | Director Calls Shots from Production Control Room | In-Studio Cameras Film Action on Set | Microphones Record Sound | Set Designed for Broadcasts to Start on Director's Call |

TRANSMITTER

Bigger, Not Better

In 1924, Scottish inventor John Logie Baird became the first person to send a picture using radio waves. He built what is considered the first TV set, complete with moving parts and its own large transmitter. Research engineers at General Electric and AT&T scrambled to improve upon the mechanical system, but it had poor picture quality.

It was soon replaced with an electronic model created in the United States by Philo T. Farnsworth. At age 14, Farnsworth began to think about how his TV invention would work. As he repeatedly plowed back and forth over his father's potato field, Farnsworth imagined that lines of light could be scanned similarly onto a picture tube. Just six years later, on September 7, 1927, Farnsworth transmitted the image of a horizontal line across the room of his San Francisco, California, lab using the scanning system still in use in today's TVs.

Turn on the TV   25

| Turn on the TV | Images Appear on Screen | Light Rays Form Inside TV | Electricity Provides Heat to TV as Receiver Picks Up Signal | Large Broadcast Dishes Send Signals to Home-Based Receivers | Space Satellites Send Signals to Broadcast Dishes | Transmitters Send Signals to Satellites |

Master Control Room Sends Signals out of TV Station

Where in the TV station do the transmitter's signals come from?

All signals sent to the transmitter come from the station's master control room. A control room is where people in charge of creating and broadcasting TV programs make decisions and give instructions. The master control room is where everything comes together.

In the master control room, the audio and video signals produced inside the station are mixed together, sometimes with graphics, or computer-generated on-screen text, from another part of the station. The signals are analyzed for clarity and then combined and strengthened so they can make the journey to the transmitter. Signals from remote broadcasts—those filmed outside the TV station—are also sent here before transmitters send them out.

Where do the signals produced in the master control room come from?

26 STEP BACK SCIENCE

| Wires Send Signals to Transmitter | **Master Control Room Sends Signals out of TV Station** | Three Control Rooms Send Signals to Master Control Room | Director Calls Shots from Production Control Room | In-Studio Cameras Film Action on Set | Microphones Record Sound | Set Designed for Broadcasts to Start on Director's Call |

▲ *The master control room sends signals from the studio to a transmitter.*

Share and Share Alike

With so much importance placed on what happens in the master control room, it is hard to believe any TV station would share this essential room with another station. That is, however, exactly what some stations do. Local and public stations in Denver, Indianapolis, New York, Philadelphia, and New Orleans have all begun to double or even triple up to decrease the cost of running their own control rooms full-time. This allows the stations to cut back on staff and save money on standby emergency control room equipment that is required by the FCC, but rarely used. More stations—including some commercial stations that do not compete for viewers—are expected to begin to share facilities as the expensive, high-tech requirements for DTV signals become a must for all TV stations by 2006.

Turn on the TV 27

| Turn on the TV | Images Appear on Screen | Light Rays Form Inside TV | Electricity Provides Heat to TV as Receiver Picks Up Signal | Large Broadcast Dishes Send Signals to Home-Based Receivers | Space Satellites Send Signals to Broadcast Dishes | Transmitters Send Signals to Satellites |

Three Control Rooms Send Signals to Master Control Room

Where do the signals produced in the master control room come from?

Usually audio, video, and production have separate control rooms that create the signals that are put together in the master control room. All three rooms are important, but the production control room is especially key. That is the main place where people who plan and direct the show watch as it is being recorded to decide what will be broadcast.

As this is happening, the video control room picks up signals from the multiple cameras that are filming in the studio. The images are checked for technical quality and proper color balance, and then sent to the production control room.

At the same time, sound engineers in the audio control room check the quality of sound being produced in the studio. They use sensitive equipment to eliminate any unwanted noises that microphones may pick up and to be sure that the on-screen talent, such as the actors or newscasters, can be heard clearly. Before they send the sound signal to the master control room, the engineers can also add music, laughter, and sound effects.

So who decides what will be seen and heard?

STEP BACK SCIENCE

| Wires Send Signals to Transmitter | Master Control Room Sends Signals out of TV Station | **Three Control Rooms Send Signals to Master Control Room** | Director Calls Shots from Production Control Room | In-Studio Cameras Film Action on Set | Microphones Record Sound | Set Designed for Broadcasts to Start on Director's Call |

▲ *Sound engineers use equipment in the audio control room to improve the quality of the sound recording.*

Limitless Laughter

How can a funny TV show be made even funnier? By adding laughter. That is the idea behind using laugh tracks—a recording of laughter mixed into the sound track of some TV shows.

The laugh track was first used on TV in 1950 on NBC's *The Hank McCune Show*. Critics were surprised, and not very enthusiastic. In *Variety*, the TV industry's top magazine for professionals, one critic said of the show, "there are chuckles and yucks dubbed in. Whether this induces a jovial mood in home viewers is still to be determined, but the practice may have unlimited possibilities if it's spread to include canned peals of hilarity, thunderous ovations, and gasps of sympathy."

Laugh tracks became popular on comedy and talk shows, and by the late 1960s applause tracks were also common. Attentive viewers may have heard familiar laughs and applause because many TV shows used the same tracks. While most comedy and talk shows are now filmed in front of a live audience so laugh tracks are not necessary, there are rumors that some shows sneak in laugh tracks from classic shows, including *I Love Lucy* and *The Munsters*.

| Turn on the TV | Images Appear on Screen | Light Rays Form Inside TV | Electricity Provides Heat to TV as Receiver Picks Up Signal | Large Broadcast Dishes Send Signals to Home-Based Receivers | Space Satellites Send Signals to Broadcast Dishes | Transmitters Send Signals to Satellites |

Director Calls Shots from Production Control Room

Who decides what will be seen and heard?

The TV show's director must visualize and direct how the show will look and sound. This person sits in the production control room and provides guidance on what he or she wants to see and hear on the set, which is the place where the show is actually recorded. Much of how the show will run is preplanned, often with the suggestions of other people who help produce it.

From inside the production control room, the director uses microphones and headphones to speak to everyone in the studio—from camera operators to the actors. One wall in the room is filled with TV screens that show images from the video control room of what is being filmed by each camera. This enables the director to decide which camera angle works best for each shot or scene to be broadcast. The director can also look down on the set through windows. Either way, the director is always looking at the big picture.

TV news programs offer a clear example of how direction works. Sometimes the newscaster will look straight into a camera to tell one story, but then turn his or her head to look into another camera in another direction to tell another story. This change of view is part of the director's vision. The newscaster may get the sign to turn his or her head from a manager near the set, who relays the director's commands. Alternatively, the newscaster may have looked for the camera whose red light is illuminated—a sure sign that it is the camera recording what is being broadcast.

So how do these in-studio cameras record action?

30 STEP BACK SCIENCE

| Wires Send Signals to Transmitter | Master Control Room Sends Signals out of TV Station | Three Control Rooms Send Signals to Master Control Room | **Director Calls Shots from Production Control Room** | In-Studio Cameras Film Action on Set | Microphones Record Sound | Set Designed for Broadcasts to Start on Director's Call |

▲ *Decisions on the look of the final broadcast are made in the production control room.*

Who Is Who in the Studio

DIRECTOR

PRODUCER

TECHNICAL MANAGER

In the studio and the production control room, many people help to produce TV shows. Among them are:

- the director, who gives directions to the crew on stage and behind the scenes and who is largely responsible for what is broadcast.

- the producer, who is generally in charge of the whole production staff, including the director. This person helped develop the show, decide on its length, and create its visual and sound content.

- the technical manager, who oversees the production equipment in the studio and control rooms.

Turn on the TV   31

| Turn on the TV | Images Appear on Screen | Light Rays Form Inside TV | Electricity Provides Heat to TV as Receiver Picks Up Signal | Large Broadcast Dishes Send Signals to Home-Based Receivers | Space Satellites Send Signals to Broadcast Dishes | Transmitters Send Signals to Satellites |

In-Studio Cameras Film Action on Set

How do these in-studio cameras record action?

A TV studio's camera works a lot like a TV in the sense that it needs light and electricity to operate. The camera picks up light through its lens as it focuses on the people or objects being filmed. Inside the camera, a prism divides the image coming through the lens into red, green, and blue light. Each beam strikes a chip called a charge-coupled device, or CCD. The CCDs are covered with light sensors. These sensors divide the images, striking them into hundreds of thousands of tiny elements called pixels, and measure the intensity of each one. The signals from the red, green, and blue CCDs are recombined to produce the video signal that leaves the camera. This output signal can be broadcast or stored on videotape. The audio signal is created at the same time as the video signal.

So how is sound recorded in a TV studio?

Live Aid

Early TV shows were recorded live, which meant viewers were able to see things on TV as they actually happened in the studio. Now only news and special events are generally shown live, although some are recorded "live in front of a studio audience," which simply means they were videotaped while an audience watched.

The main reason for live shows was necessity, because broadcast transmissions required live audio and video. It was not until 1956 that videotape was introduced during a press event promoted by CBS. Two years later, when it was perfected, stations across the United States were eager to use this new technology to tape shows.

STEP BACK SCIENCE

| Wires Send Signals to Transmitter | Master Control Room Sends Signals out of TV Station | Three Control Rooms Send Signals to Master Control Room | Director Calls Shots from Production Control Room | **In-Studio Cameras Film Action on Set** | Microphones Record Sound | Set Designed for Broadcasts to Start on Director's Call |

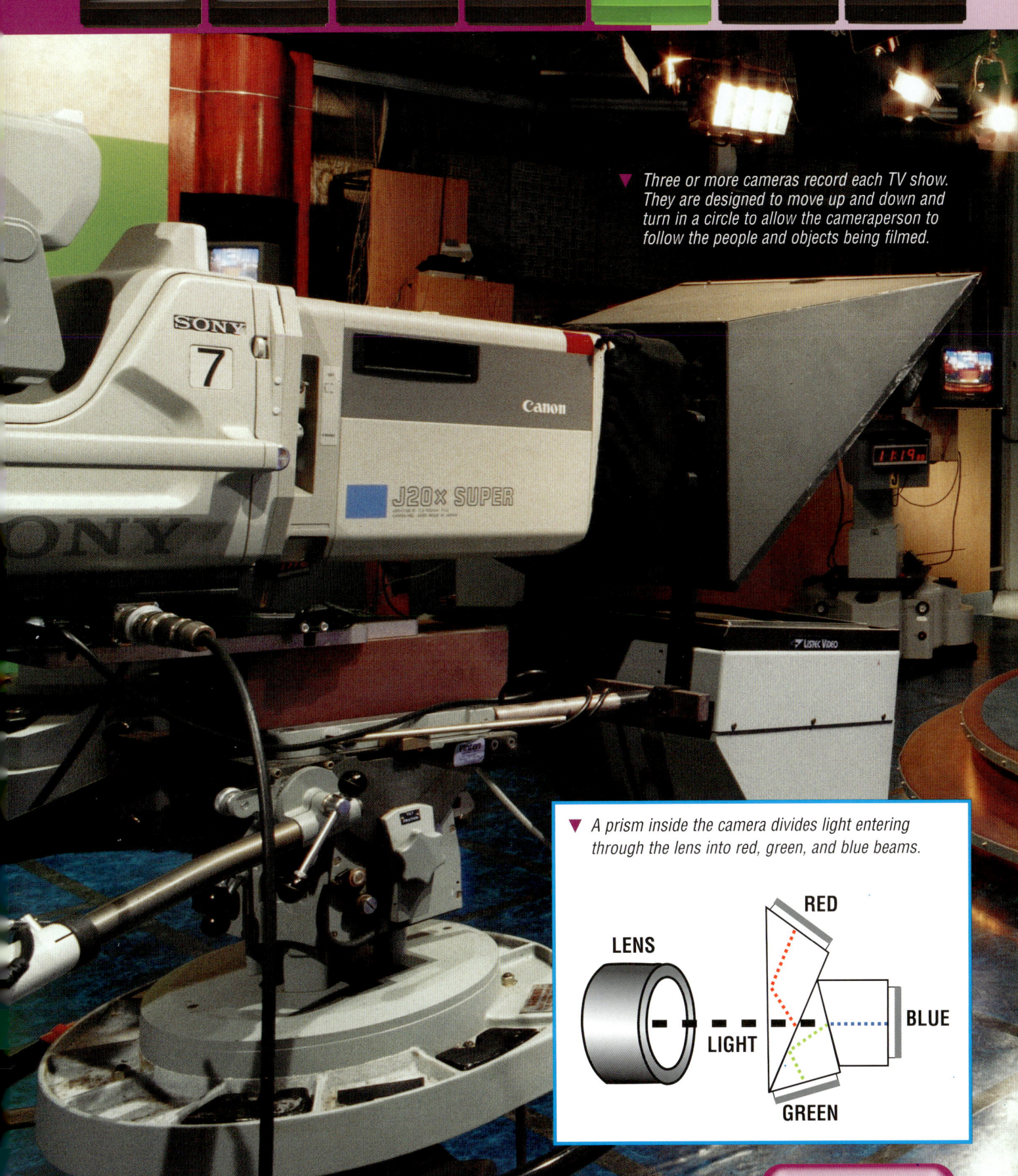

▼ *Three or more cameras record each TV show. They are designed to move up and down and turn in a circle to allow the cameraperson to follow the people and objects being filmed.*

▼ *A prism inside the camera divides light entering through the lens into red, green, and blue beams.*

LENS — LIGHT — RED / BLUE / GREEN

Turn on the TV 33

| Turn on the TV | Images Appear on Screen | Light Rays Form Inside TV | Electricity Provides Heat to TV as Receiver Picks Up Signal | Large Broadcast Dishes Send Signals to Home-Based Receivers | Space Satellites Send Signals to Broadcast Dishes | Transmitters Send Signals to Satellites |

Microphones Record Sound

How is sound recorded in a TV studio?

Like images, sound needs to change form to flow through wires. Sound created on the set is recorded through microphones. One of the most commonly used microphone styles is the boom, a microphone that is mounted on a long arm so that it can be held out of a TV shot, above the people on-screen.

Inside a microphone, sound waves cause a thin disk, the diaphragm, to vibrate. The moving diaphragm activates a coil near a magnet. Because the microphone is attached to an electrical outlet, the moving diaphragm and magnet make tiny amounts of electricity flow through the microphone in the same pattern as the sound waves. In this way, sound energy is converted to electrical energy. These electrical waves create the signal that flows through the microphone wires to the sound control room.

So where in a TV studio are the picture and sound produced?

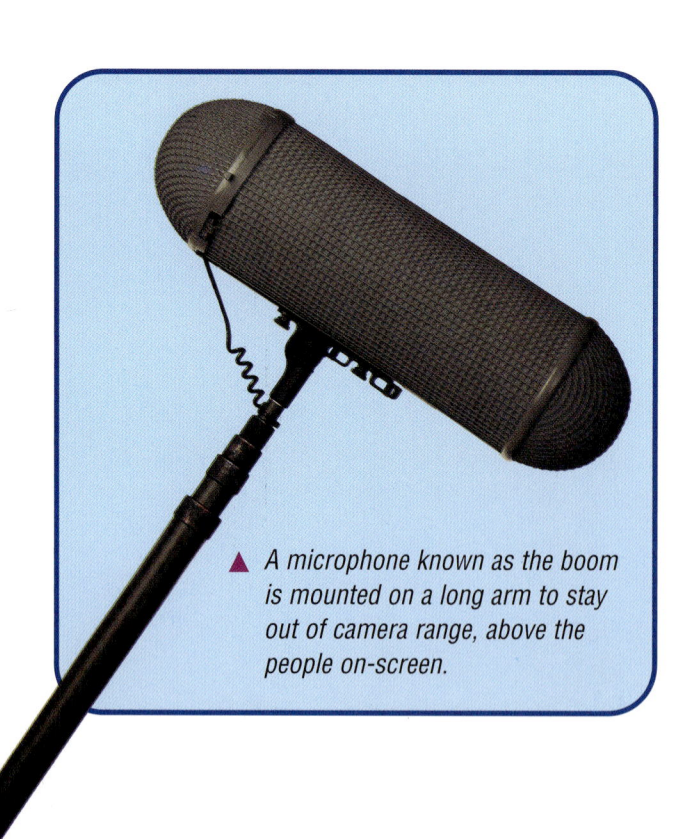

▲ A microphone known as the boom is mounted on a long arm to stay out of camera range, above the people on-screen.

34 STEP BACK SCIENCE

| Wires Send Signals to Transmitter | Master Control Room Sends Signals out of TV Station | Three Control Rooms Send Signals to Master Control Room | Director Calls Shots from Production Control Room | In-Studio Cameras Film Action on Set | **Microphones Record Sound** | Set Designed for Broadcasts to Start on Director's Call |

- diaphragm
- magnet
- wire coil

▲ *A microphone converts sound waves into electrical signals.*

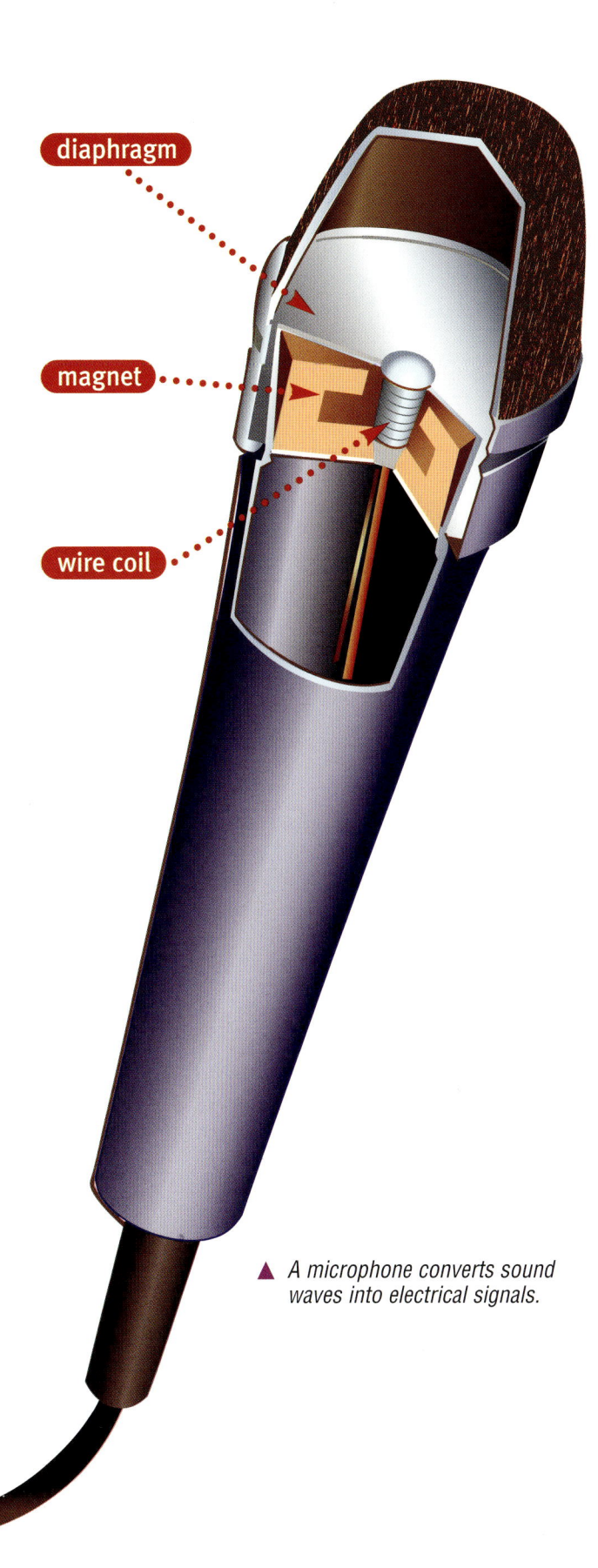

▲ *A telegraph operator's technique led to the development of the microphone.*

Microphone Magic

In 1870, at age nineteen, German-born Emile Berliner moved to Washington, D.C., to study physics part-time. At the time, telegraphs were the main form of communication. These machines transmitted and received simple electric impulses through wires by analyzing and translating a code of keyboard taps produced by the message maker.

Berliner learned from a telegraph operator that the harder the user tapped on the key, the more electrical current would pass through the machine. With this principle in mind, Berliner made a special transmitter. This new transmitter varied the amount of contact pressure between the terminals (beginning and end points of an electrical circuit) when a sound with different degrees of intensity, such as a voice, acted against it. By age twenty-five, Berliner created the microphone, which he sold for fifty thousand dollars to the Bell Telephone Company.

Turn on the TV

Side Step

REMOTE CONTROL

How is the creation of video footage different outside a studio?

▲ Television equipment used on location is designed for easy portability.

Studio cameras and the handheld cameras used by TV crews "on location" are very similar. They both use CCD technology to turn light images into electrical signals for broadcast. The main difference between studio equipment and field equipment is the field equipment's ability to travel.

Handheld cameras are lightweight, weighing as little as a few pounds. They can be placed on portable tripods for stability or, if necessary, they can ride on the cameraperson's shoulder. When electrical outlets are in short supply, or if long cables would be too inconvenient, they can draw their power from batteries. They can also record their images directly onto videotapes stored in the body of the camera. These videotapes can be brought back to the main studio for editing, or they can be edited in the mobile studio in the station's news van. Vans can also transmit their footage back to the studio via satellite, using satellite dishes mounted on their roofs, like those below.

›› JONES ROUNDS THIRD AHEAD OF THE THROW. IF HE SCORES THAT WILL MAKE IT 2-1 FOR THE BULLDOGS

▲ Closed captions present spoken words and sounds on-screen as they happen.

Read All About It

Closed captioning has opened the world of TV to many people. In closed captioning, words and sounds typically heard by viewers are typed as text on the bottom of the TV screen.

Although closed captioning was originally created for use by the deaf, a federal law now states that all TVs 13 inches or larger built after 1993 must include closed-captioning decoders. The decoders enable the TV screen to display the captions, which are provided as part of the signal sent to the set. The captions are usually typed in at the television station or added by an outside company. Live shows can be captioned as they happen, printed on-screen just a few seconds behind what is being said and shown. The typist listens to the broadcast and types the words into a special computer program that adds the captions to the television signal.

Turn on the TV   37

| Turn on the TV | Images Appear on Screen | Light Rays Form Inside TV | Electricity Provides Heat to TV as Receiver Picks Up Signal | Large Broadcast Dishes Send Signals to Home-Based Receivers | Space Satellites Send Signals to Broadcast Dishes | Transmitters Send Signals to Satellites |

Set Designed for Broadcasts to Start on Director's Call

Where in a TV studio are the picture and sound produced?

They are produced in a place called a set. The set is designed to make broadcasts run as smoothly as possible, but nothing is broadcast until the director gives a sign that everything is ready for action to begin. Usually the set has no windows to the outdoors, and thick walls keep out distracting sounds and light. Powerful lights that hang from the ceiling are positioned to brighten every part of the set being filmed—after all, light is needed not just for viewing but also for filming. Once the on-screen talent is on the set and all equipment is in place to translate light images and sound waves into electrical signals, the director will check with people in the studio to make sure that everything is in working order. Then the director will call "action" or give a hand signal, so action starts on the set as cameras roll.

▲ A cameraman at work

Talent Show

The anchorpeople, newscasters, talk show hosts, and actors who appear on-screen, also known as the talent, are the people audiences see and come to recognize. But behind the scenes are many others whose work is important to producing a TV show. A floor manager wears earphones to hear a director's comments, which he or she relays to the talent. Prop managers take care of scenery and props. Stagehands move props and scenery around the soundstage to improve shots. A camera operator controls the camera's focus and point of view. A lighting director makes sure the stage is properly lit.

38 STEP BACK SCIENCE

| Wires Send Signals to Transmitter | Master Control Room Sends Signals out of TV Station | Three Control Rooms Send Signals to Master Control Room | Director Calls Shots from Production Control Room | In-Studio Cameras Film Action on Set | Microphones Record Sound | **Set Designed for Broadcasts to Start on Director's Call** |

▲ The set is where action takes place and is recorded in sound and pictures.

Turn on the TV 39

The Big Picture

Explore the science behind turning on the TV, step by step:

14 Turn on the TV
Turn on the TV to see images and hear sound.
(pages 6–7)

12 Light Rays Form Inside TV
The heating of the cathode part of the cathode-ray tube creates electrons.
(pages 10–11)

9 Space Satellites Bounce Signals Back to Earth
Dishes on Earth receive signals from a satellite in space.
(pages 20–21)

13 Images Appear on Screen
Electrons shoot through the shadow mask and hit the phosphor dot screen, which produces light that is seen as images on the screen.
(pages 8–9)

11 Electricity Provides Heat to TV as Receiver Picks Up Signal
Electricity enters the TV through a wire and heats the cathode. At the same time, the receiver outside the home picks up audio and video signals in the form of radio waves.
(pages 12–13)

10 Large Broadcast Dishes Send Signals to Home-Based Receivers
Broadcast dishes near local TV and cable stations send signal to home receivers.
(pages 16–17)

40 STEP BACK SCIENCE

8 Transmitters Send Signals to Satellites

Transmitters located near TV stations send the signals, which hit the satellite.
(pages 22–23)

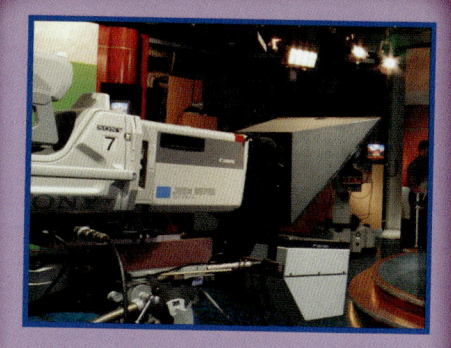

3 In-Studio Cameras Film Action on Set

The cameras are designed to change light images into electrical signals.
(pages 32–33)

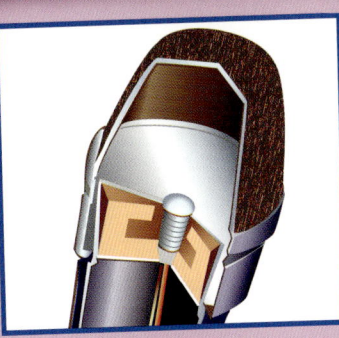

2 Microphones Record Sound

Microphones turn sound waves into electrical signals.
(pages 34–35)

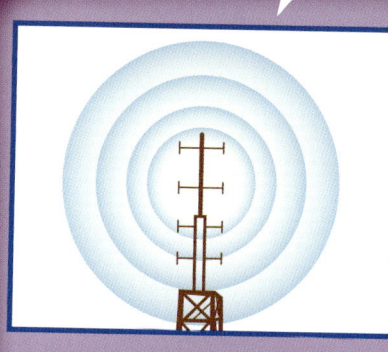

7 Wires Send Signals to Transmitter

TV signals reach the transmitter through wire cables from the TV station.
(pages 24–25)

4 Director Calls Shots from Production Control Room

The director watches action on set and relays commands to the stage to be sure the broadcast meets its pre-planned needs.
(pages 30–31)

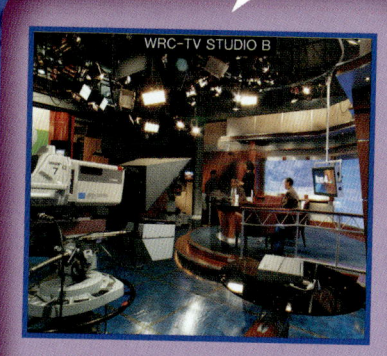

1 Set Designed for Broadcasts to Start on Director's Call

Thick, windowless walls and bright lighting are part of a set. Broadcast from the stage starts when the director determines that everything on the stage is ready.
(pages 38–39)

6 Master Control Room Sends Signals out of TV Station

The master control room acts as a nerve center of the station, putting together and sending out a collective audio/video signal.
(pages 26–27)

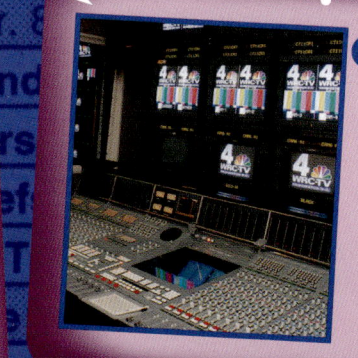

5 Three Control Rooms Send Signals to Master Control Room

Signals are produced in three control rooms: production (where people direct the show's action), audio (where sound is checked for clarity and additional sounds, such as music, may be added), and video (where the images are checked for clarity and color).
(pages 28–29)

Turn on the TV 41

Facts and Figures
Seen and Heard

TV Time: Many inventors from around the world helped make TV possible, often by building on each other's ideas.

1603	1745	1831	1837
Italian Vincenzo Cascariolo discovers that substances called phosphors will glow when light shines on them.	William Watson sends an electric charge through a 2-mile-long metal wire in his laboratory in England.	Englishman Michael Faraday creates a machine to generate electricity.	Samuel Morse invents the telegraph, which sends electrical signals over great distances, in the United States. Meanwhile in England, James Clerk Maxwell discovers that light travels in waves.

Telegraph ▶

1901	1906	1907	1918
Italian Guglielmo Marconi, inventor of radio, sends sound across the Atlantic Ocean by way of radio waves.	In the United States, Lee de Forest discovers a way to amplify an electrical signal.	Russian Boris Rosing uses a cathode-ray tube to reproduce images.	American Edwin Howard Armstrong perfects a way of amplifying radio waves.

Marconi ▶

First in Line

W2XB, a television station formed in 1928 by General Electric (GE), was the first station to operate in the United States, and today it is the world's oldest continually operating TV station. In March 1942, it was renamed WRGB to honor former GE vice president Dr. Walter R.G. Baker, but under both names it has made a lot of TV history. The station boasts the first:
- TV newscaster in the United States. Anchor Kolin Hager broadcast farm and weather reports three times a week, beginning May 10, 1928.
- dramatic program for American viewers. "The Queen's Messenger" used three cameras to broadcast to four TV sets in September 1928.
- airing of a TV commercial in June 1946. The ad was for Gillette Razors, which sponsored a boxing match between Joe Louis and Bill Conn.

42 STEP BACK SCIENCE

1876
In the United States, Emile Berliner invents the microphone, which changes sound waves into electricity. In the next few years, Alexander Graham Bell and Thomas Edison improve on the design. Also, Thomas Edison invents the phonograph and, a year later, moving pictures (movies without sound).

1878
Englishman William Crookes invents the first cathode-ray tube. An improved one is designed by K.F. Braun of Germany in 1887.

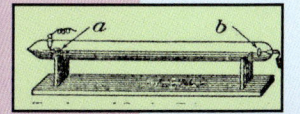

Crookes (left) and the cathode-ray tube (bottom)

Early 1880s
Heinrich Hertz of Germany discovers how to create radio waves and send them through space at the speed of light.

1884
In Germany, Paul Nipkow invents a mechanical scanning disk that breaks images into little dots of light that can produce electricity.

1924–29
Scotsman John Baird sends sound and pictures mechanically from England to the United States.

1927
AT&T scientists send pictures and sound from New York City to Washington, D.C., using a mechanical scanning disc. American J.A. O'Neil creates magnetic tape to record sound.

1927
American Philo T. Farnsworth transmits an image of a horizontal line across his room, using an electronic TV camera tube and a TV receiver tube.

1929
Russian-born Vladimir Zworykin patents his own version of an electronic TV camera tube and a TV receiver tube in the United States.

1948
Three American scientists at Bell Laboratories invent transistors.

SET TO SELL
America's first mass-produced TV set was a Dumont model, which was put on the market in 1938. The set sat in a walnut cabinet, had a 15-inch-wide screen, and cost $395. In advertisements, the company claimed that its models were the "first commercial television receivers for home use." The TV's maker, Allen Du Mont, got a jump on other TV manufacturers because he visited England in late 1936 and sent one of their set models—brand new and not yet used in homes—back to the United States.

Color Them Late
By September 1962, color TV's popularity was growing in America. The NBC network was broadcasting 68 percent of the shows on its schedule in color when ABC finally began to broadcast in color too. The CBS network aired all its shows in black and white until December 1967.

◀ *Early NBC logo*

Turn on the TV   43

Wonders and Words

Questions and Answers

Q: *Can people block certain TV stations from transmitting into their homes?*

A: Since 1999, newly built TV sets larger than 13 inches sold in the United States must contain a V-chip. The V-chip ("V" for "violence") was designed to allow parents to cut off the transmissions of specific TV shows into their homes. Besides audio and video, every signal also includes information about each show's rating, which can be read by the chip. Each TV can be programmed with a rating, so that the TV will block all shows above that rating. Here are the ratings:

- **TV-Y** Children as young as 2 can watch; zero violence or sexual content
- **TV-Y7** For children 7 and over; may contain mild violence
- **TV-G** For general audiences; little or no sex, violence, or inappropriate language
- **TV-PG** Parental guidance suggested
- **TV-14** Suitable only for people over 14; some sex or violence
- **TV-MA** Suitable only for mature audiences; may contain graphic violence or sexual situations

Q: *How does videotape work?*

A: Videotape is plastic tape with a light-sensitive coating that records light images. Before being broadcast, the film is run through a machine that converts the film's light images into signals that can be transmitted. Videotape is recorded in three sections: the control track, the sound track, and the video track. Each track is recorded on a different part of the tape. The control track, which controls the number of images per second, takes up the top part of the tape. The sound track, a band of audio signal, is placed below it. The video, or picture, track is recorded diagonally across the middle of the tape.

Q: *What is WebTV?*

A: WebTV is the Internet on a TV screen. It works with the installation of a TV Internet receiver (instead of a TV antenna) that is connected to a TV and a phone line for Internet access. The receiver picks up Internet and TV signals, allowing the viewer to switch between surfing the Internet and watching TV on the same screen.

Glossary

Amplify: strengthen

Audio signal: an electrical signal that carries sound data, which is converted back into sound in a TV set

Broadcast: cast over a broad area; also a term for a show transmitted to TV sets, or the signal that is sent out into the atmosphere

Cables: protected wires that carry audio and video signals

Cathode-ray tube: a closed glass tube in which electrons flow before hitting a screen and making parts of it glow

Control room: place from which directions are sent in a TV studio

Down-linking: sending a signal from a satellite to Earth

Fiber Optics: threadlike glass or plastic cables through which light waves carrying audio and video signals can flow

Frequency: in general, the number of times a wave of energy moves up and down in a second; each TV channel has its own frequency, and each one is picked up by antennas tuned into the unique frequency

Phosphor: a chemical that glows when light strikes it

Photoelectric effect: the phenomenon of light striking something and producing electricity

Radio waves: electromagnetic waves of a specific energy level

Remote broadcast: a broadcast originating away from a TV studio

Satellite: a human-made object sent into space by a rocket and released above Earth so it can be used to transmit signals

Scanning: moving back and forth, as in the movement of a light beam across the screen of a cathode-ray tube

Shot: a scene shown through the camera

Sound wave: a compression wave caused by a vibrating object

Transmitter: a device that sends out broadcast signals

Transistor: a tiny device that can direct, control, and amplify signals

Up-linking: sending a signal from Earth to a satellite in space

Video signal: an electronic or radio signal that can be converted into images

Index

ABC *(American Broadcasting Company)*, 16, 43

Antenna, 12, 16, 19, 25, 44

Armstrong, Edwin Howard, 42

AT&T (American Telephone and Telegraph Company), 25, 43

Baird, John Logie, 25, 43

Baker, Walter R.G., 42

Bardeen, John, 10

Bell, Alexander Graham, 43

Bell Telephone Company, 10, 35, 43

Berliner, Emile, 35, 43

Brattain, Walter, 10

Braun, K.F., 43

Broadcast dishes, 16, 17, 20, 40

Cable television, 12, 18, 19, 21

Cascariolo, Vincenzo, 42

Cathode-ray tube, 9, 10, 11, 32, 40, 42, 43, 45

CBS (Central Broadcasting Service), 16, 43

Crookes, William, 43

De Forest, Lee, 38

Denver (Colorado), 27

Diaphragm, 34, 35

Director, television, 30, 31, 38, 41

Du Mont, Allen, 43

Edison, Thomas, 43

Electricity, 10, 12, 14, 15, 32, 35, 40

Electrons, 8, 9, 10, 11, 32, 37, 40

Empire State Building, 15, 16

Faraday, Michael, 42

Farnsworth, Philo T., 25, 43

FCC (Federal Communications Commission), 22, 27

Fiber-optic cable, 12, 16, 21, 45

General Electric company, 25, 42

Germanium (element), 10

Hager, Kolin, 42

HBO (Home Box Office), 19

Heat, 10, 12

Hertz, Heinrich, 43

Indianapolis (Indiana), 27

Internet, 44

Light, speed of, 18, 43

Magnet, 10, 34, 35

Manager, television, 30, 31

Marconi, Guglielmo, 42

Maxwell, James Clerk, 42

Microphones, 28, 30, 34, 35, 37, 41, 43

Morse, Samuel, 42

NBC *(National Broadcasting Company)*, 18, 43

New Orleans (Louisiana), 27

New York City, 13, 15, 16, 27, 43

Nipkow, Paul, 43

O'Neil, J.A., 43

Philadelphia (Pennsylvania), 27

Phosphors, 8, 9, 22, 40, 42, 45

Picture Tube. See *Cathode-ray tube*

Producer, television, 31

Radio waves, 12, 13, 15, 16, 18, 20, 22, 23, 25, 40, 42, 43, 45
Receiver, 6, 12, 16, 37, 40
Remote control, 14, 15
Roosevelt, Franklin D., 13
Rosing, Boris, 42

San Francisco (California), 25
Satellite dish, 12, 13, 18, 19
Satellites, 6, 19, 20, 21, 22, 40, 41, 45
Shadow mask, 8, 10, 11
Shockley, William, 10
Signals
    audio, 12, 24, 26, 28, 32, 40, 41, 44, 45
    broadcast, 6, 12, 18, 37
    electrical, 14, 15, 16, 22, 24, 35, 37, 41, 42
    light, 12, 18

television, 6, 9, 12, 13, 16, 20, 21, 22, 24, 41
video, 12, 24, 26, 28, 32, 40, 41, 44, 45
Sound waves, 34, 35, 41, 45

Telegraph, 35, 42
Television, 6, 9, 12, 22, 44
    black-and-white, 9
    camera, 30, 32, 33, 36, 37, 41, 43
    digital, 22, 27
    history and invention of, 9, 13, 15, 25, 43
    how it works, 8, 12
    parts of, 11, 12
    screen, 8, 40
Television station, 6, 16, 21, 22, 23, 24, 26, 27, 37, 40, 41, 44
    control room, 26, 27, 28, 29, 30, 34, 41, 45

set, 38, 39, 41
studio, 28, 30, 38
Transistor, 10, 43, 45
Transmitters, 6, 22, 23, 24, 25, 26, 35, 41, 44
TV. See *Television*

Video taping, 32, 37, 44

Washington, D.C., 35, 43
Watson, William, 42
WebTV, 44
Wilkes-Barre (Pennsylvania), 19
World Trade Center, 16
WRGB (TV station), 42

Zworykin, Vladimir, 43

Credits:

Produced by: J.A. Ball Associates, Inc.
Jacqueline Ball, Justine Ciovacco, Andrew Willett
Daniel H. Franck, Ph.D., Science Consultant

Art Direction, Design, and Production:
designlabnyc
Todd Cooper, Sonia Gauba, Jay Jaffe

Writer: Justine Ciovacco

Cover: Brooke Fasani: boy with TV; Ablestock/Hemera: RGB phosphors; PhotoDisc, Inc.: satellite dishes and antenna, production control room; Courtesy of Communications Engineering Inc.: set.

Interior: Brooke Fasani: pp.6–7 boy with TV, old TV; PhotoDisc, Inc.: p.9 girl on TV, p.13 satellite dishes and antenna, p.21 satellite, fiber-optic cable, p.23 transmitter, p.31 production control room, p.32 videotape, p.36 cameraman, p.37 news vans with satellite dishes; Sonia "On/Off" Gauba: p.11 diagram of picture tube, pp.24–25 diagram of TV signal transmission, pp.35–36 diagram of microphone; Library of Congress: p.13 news broadcast, p.25 Philo T. Farnsworth; John Garbarini Photography: p.14 remote controls; Photospin: p.15 Empire State Building; Ablestock/Hemera: p.9 RGB phosphors, p.16 World Trade Center antenna, p.17 broad dish, p.35 boom microphone, p.35 telegraph; Courtesy of RCN: cable worker; ©DirectTV, Inc.: p.22 directTV logo; Courtesy of Communications Engineering Inc.: p.27 master control room, p.29 audio control room, p.33 camera, p.39 set; Jay Jaffe: p.33 diagram of camera; p.37 closed captioned image; ArtToday: p.38 cameraman, p.40 Marconi, telegraph, GE logo, p.39 Crookes, cathode-ray tube, old tv, old NBC logo.

Special thanks to Ed Drabik/Communications Engineering Inc.

For More Information

www.tvhistory.tv
Television History—The First 75 Years
This site gives time lines and photos of the history of TV broadcasting, broadcast technology, and television sets.

entertainment.howstuffworks.com/tv.htm
How Stuff Works—How Television Works
This site explains how televisions work. Links in its articles will lead you to information on VCRs and DVD players, cable broadcasting, and much more.

Bendick, Jeanne and Robert **Eureka! It's Television!** Brookfield, CT: Millbrook Press, 1993.

Fisher, David E., and Marshall J. Fisher. **Tube: The Invention of Television.** New York: Counterpoint, 1988. Reprint, Collingdale, PA: Diane, 1999.